Lilian Edvall

Pictures by Anna-Clara Tidholm

THE RABBIT
WHO LONGED FOR HOME

Translated by
Elisabeth Kallick Dyssegaard

R&S
BOOKS

Stockholm New York London Adelaide Toronto

To Nils

JP

Rabén and Sjögren Bokförlag
www.raben.se

Translation copyright © 2001 by Rabén and Sjögren
All rights reserved
Originally published in Sweden by Rabén and Sjögren Bokförlag
under the title *Kaninen som längtade hem*, text copyright © 1999 by Lilian Edvall
Illustrations copyright © 1999 by Anna-Clara Tidholm
Library of Congress card number 2001 130142
Printed in Denmark
First American edition, 2001

ISBN 91-29-65391-6

*Rabén & Sjögren Bokförlag is part of P. A. Norstedt & Söner AB,
established in 1823*

Once upon a time there was a rabbit who was terribly afraid of going to day care.
More than anything, the rabbit wanted to stay home and sleep all morning and play all afternoon.

But as it happened, the rabbit's mommy and daddy both went off to work every day, so he *had* to go to day care.
One day the rabbit came up with a sneaky plan.
If he hid under the bed, no one would see him.

Oh well, off he went to day care.

The rabbit was the shyest of all the rabbits at day care.
He never wanted his mommy or his daddy to leave
him. He held on to their paws very, very tightly.

When they left, he did not let go.

The rabbit cried and looked at the door long
after Mommy and Daddy had disappeared.

And he went over to the window to see if they
might already be coming to pick him up.

The rabbit was a bit scared of the rabbit teachers. They looked stern, and they made sure that all the rabbit kids ate their carrots.

He was also a little afraid of the other kids.

But once in a while the rabbit would
forget that he was longing for home.

Then the rabbit teachers thought he was doing very well.
Mommy and Daddy were also happy.
Everyone hoped that now the rabbit would have fun at
day care just like the other kids.

But the next day it was the same old story.
The rabbit cried in the morning. Later he spent the
day waiting for his mommy and daddy.

Time passed for the rabbit who more than anything
wanted to sleep all morning and play all afternoon.
Until one day, a completely ordinary day in the middle of
the week, a new rabbit teacher came to day care. She
had unusually long ears. The rabbit thought she was the
prettiest rabbit he had ever seen, besides his mommy.

She was also nice. Every morning he got to sit on
her lap for a long time.

One day, when he had sat there for a while, he
noticed that his feet were beginning to itch.
He felt like jumping down and playing.

Another day there was already a rabbit sitting
on her lap. Now he got to sit next to her and
help her make the unhappy rabbit feel better.
He patted the kid's little paw and said, "Mommy
is coming soon."

A third day the rabbit laughed loudest of all when one of the teachers read a silly story at circle time.

But the funniest thing happened
a few weeks later . . .

It was the afternoon that Mommy and Daddy told
him the Big News.
Soon the rabbit was going to have a little brother or a
little sister.
Either Mommy or Daddy was going to be at home.
He would no longer have to go to day care!

Then suddenly the rabbit didn't
know if he was sad or glad.